D1037915

DRAGONBLOOD

DRAGON COWBOY

BY MICHAEL DAHL

ILLUSTRATED BY
FEDERICO PIATTI

STONE ARCH BOOKS
a capstone imprint

Zone Books are published by
Stone Arch Books
A Capstone Imprint
151 Good Counsel Drive, P.O. Box 669
Mankato, Minnesota 56002
www.capstonepub.com

Library of Congress Cataloging-in-Publication Data is
available on the Library of Congress website.

Library binding: 978-1-4342-1927-5

Art Director: Kay Fraser
Graphic Designer: Hilary Wacholz
Production Specialist: Michelle Biedscheid

TABLE OF CONTENTS

Introduction

A new Age of Dragons is about to begin. The **powerful** creatures will return to rule the **world** once more, but this time will be different. This time, they will have allies. Who will help them? Around the world, some young humans are making a strange discovery. They are learning that they were born with dragon blood – blood that gives them **amazing powers.**

CHAPTER 1
STAMPEDE

In a deep valley in Wyoming, a teenage boy _rode_ his horse.

The cowboy was working on a ranch for the summer.

Some cattle had **WANDERED**
off that afternoon.

He thought he saw them heading
toward the valley.

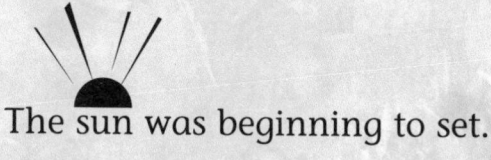

The sun was beginning to set.

Slowly, shadows **climbed** the walls on either side.

The **sky** turned purple.

The horse snorted. It was nervous.

"What's wrong, boy?" asked the cowboy. "Do you smell those cattle?"

The **missing** cattle suddenly appeared. They rushed from around the valley's **rocky** wall.

Their hooves **pounded** against the dark valley floor.

What's wrong with them? wondered the cowboy.

Then he saw a reddish light **blazing** behind the rocks.

A **towering** shadow appeared above the cowboy and his horse.

The shadow's **WINGS** blotted out the stars.

FIRE ROARED from its mouth.

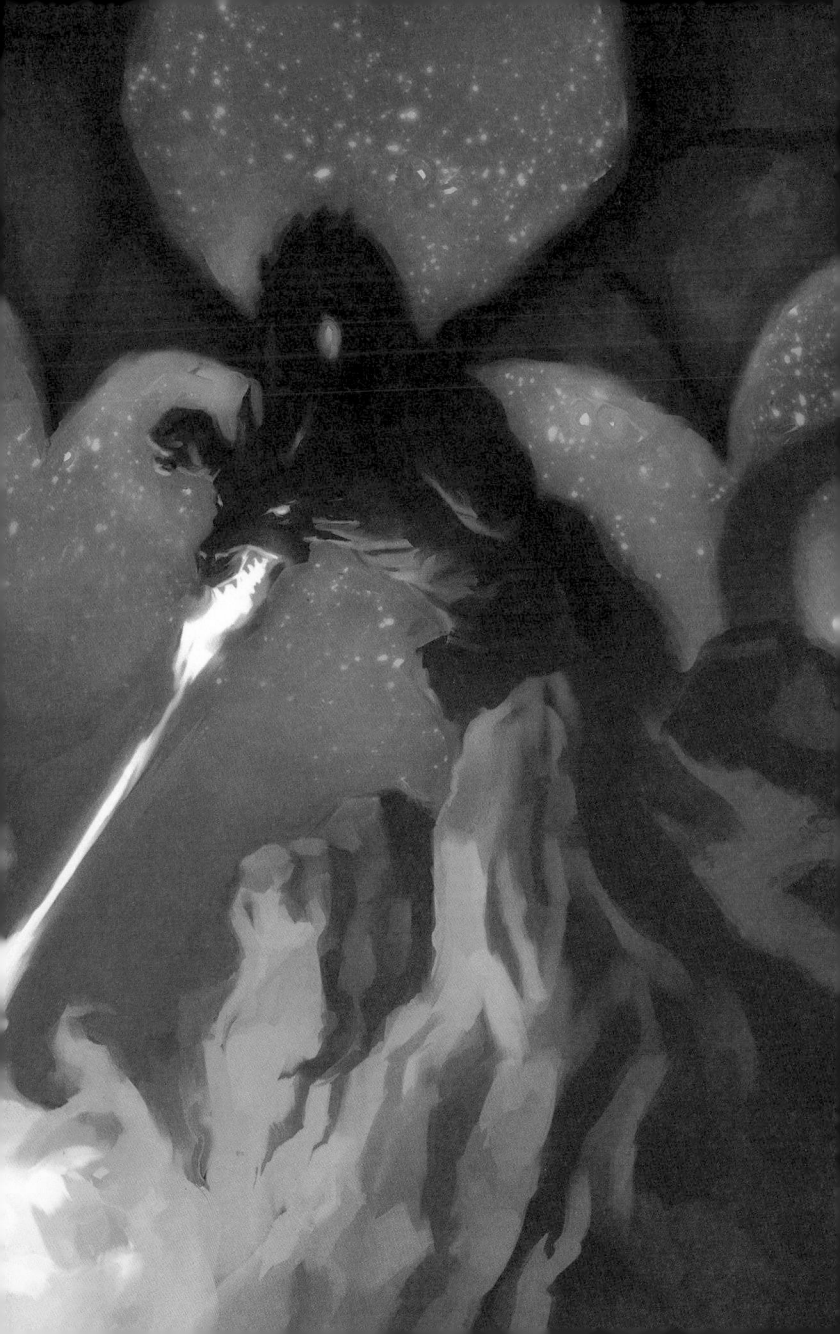

CHAPTER 2
THE STRANGER

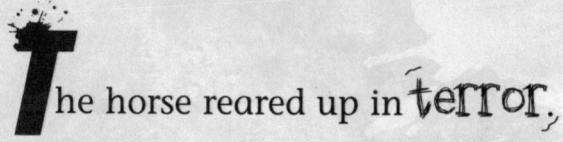he horse reared up in terror.

The cowboy **GRIPPED** the reins.

The **shadow** grew smaller.

As the cowboy watched, the shadow seemed to sink into the ground.

The boy jumped off his horse.

He **walked** over to where the shadow had vanished.

A **stranger** lay on the ground.

It was a teenage boy. **Steam** rose
from his skin. A **BIRTHMARK**, shaped
like a dragon, glowed on his arm.

CHAPTER 3
HIDING

The boy on the ground opened his eyes.

For a second, they looked like the eyes of a lizard.

Then he BLINKED, and his eyes were normal.

"I'm so cold," said the strange boy.

The cowboy **HELPED** the stranger onto his horse. Then he climbed up behind him.

An **hour** later, the horse reached one of the ranch's barns.

"You can stay here," said the cowboy. "No one will bother you out here."

"Thanks," said the stranger. His voice sounded weak.

As the cowboy walked toward the door, he **stopped**.

The **strange** boy was already asleep.

His dragon birthmark had stopped **glowing**.

Then the cowboy began to **scratch** his arm.

He pulled up his sleeve.

His own **BIRTHMARK** was
bothering him again.

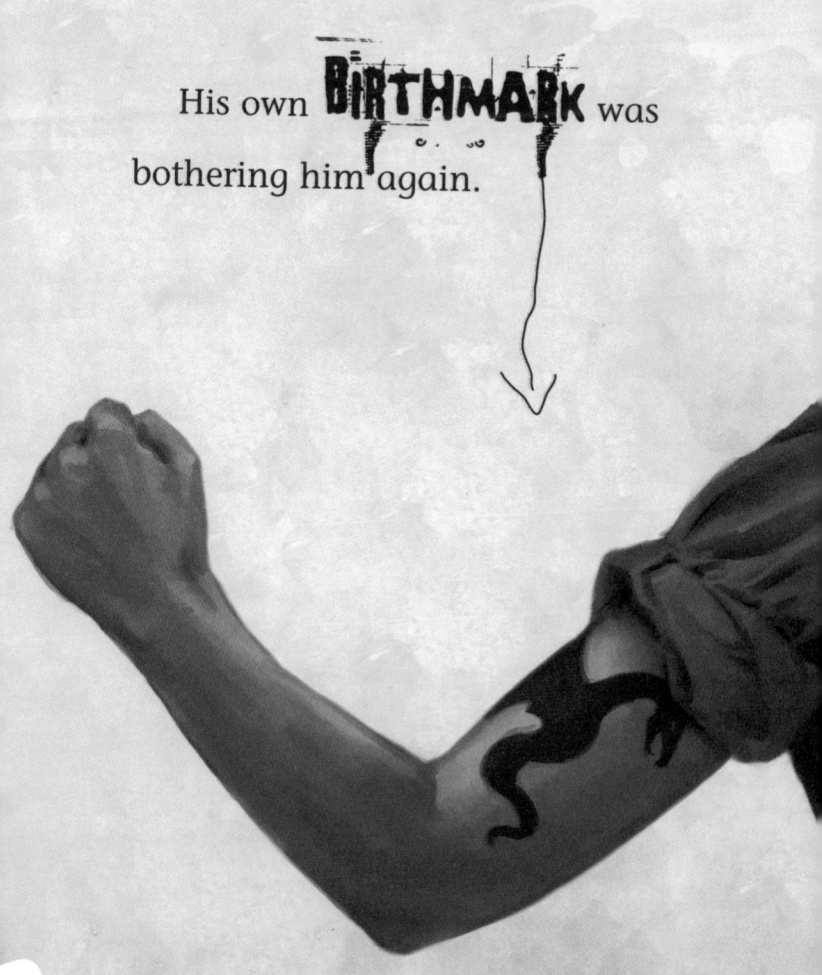

CHAPTER 4
NIGHT FLIGHT

That night, the COWBOY lay awake in his bed.

For many years, he had read books about dragons. The books were full of SCALES and wings and fire.

His father had always laughed at the books. "You're wasting your time with this garbage," his father had told him. "You need to grow up."

That was why the cowboy was working on the **ranch** that summer. His father thought it would be good for him.

"You'll be doing real work," his father had said, "and not daydreaming about **MONSTERS**."

The cowboy heard a noise. He sat up and looked out the window at the barn.

A strange **reddish** light glowed in its windows.

The cowboy *rushed* outside.

The strange boy was **gone**, but the barn **wasn't** empty.

A dragon stood before him with **BLAZING** eyes.

"I know it's you," said the cowboy.

The dragon **bent** its head and scratched with its claws in the dirt.

It wrote letters: H E N R Y

The cowboy pulled up his sleeve and showed the dragon his **ARM**.

"Look, Henry!" he cried. "I'm the same. I'm like you. But I can't fly!"

The dragon lowered itself to the ground. He **NODDED** toward his scaly back.

The cowboy's eyes **grew** wide.

Then he quickly jumped onto the creature's back as if it were his own horse.

UP and UP the monster flew.

The cowboy looked down at the ranch in the MOONLIGHT.

His father had been right. It was a good idea to come here.

Cowboy Clothing and Gear

A hat was an important tool for any cowboy. It was used as an umbrella when it rained, for shade in the hot sun, and to carry water to his horse.

Some cowboys wore **leather** cuffs around their wrists. This would protect them from injuries. Some cowboys also wore gloves.

A cowboy would often wear a bandanna around his neck. It was called a **neckerchief**. This was a very useful tool. It could be used as a washcloth, a towel, a hot pad, a bandage, or a sling. It was also used to keep dust out of a cowboy's nose and mouth.

Cowboy **boots** didn't always have a pointy toe. In fact, early cowboy boots had square toes. The boots could be worn on either foot. A cowboy would have to mold them to his feet by getting them wet and walking around until they fit.

A **vest** was another common piece of cowboy clothing. It was made of leather, canvas, or wool and used for warmth on cold nights. The pockets were very useful for storing small items like buffalo teeth and arrowheads.

Every cowboy carried a rope, and learning to throw it was a must. In order to catch an animal, a cowboy had to throw the **ROPE** while on ground and on his horse.

ABOUT THE AUTHOR

Michael Dahl is the author of more than 200 books for children and young adults. He has won the AEP Distinguished Achievement Award three times for his nonfiction. His Finnegan Zwake mystery series was shortlisted twice by the Anthony and Agatha awards. He has also written the Library of Doom series. He is a featured speaker at conferences around the country on graphic novels and high-interest books for boys.

ABOUT THE ILLUSTRATOR

After getting a graphic design degree and working as a designer for a couple of years, Federico Piatti realized he was spending way too much time drawing and painting, and too much money on art books and comics, so his path took a turn toward illustration. He currently works creating imagery for books and games, mostly in the fantasy and horror genres. Argentinian by birth, he now lives in Madrid, Spain, with his wife, who is also an illustrator.

GLOSSARY

birthmark (BURTH-mark)—a mark on the skin that was there from birth

blazing (BLAYZ-ing)—burning

blotted (BLOT-tid)—blocked

cattle (KAT-uhl)—cows, bulls, and steers that are raised for food or for their hides

creature (KREE-chur)—a living being

ranch (RANCH)—a large farm for cattle, sheep, or horses

reared (RIHRD)—lifted up

reins (RAYNZ)—straps attached to a bridle to control or guide a horse

scales (SKALEZ)—small pieces of hard skin that cover the body of a reptile

valley (VAL-ee)—an area of low ground between two hills

DISCUSSION QUESTIONS

1. Why did the cowboy's father **send** him to the ranch? Talk about why sometimes parents make decisions for their kids.

2. Do you think that Henry and the cowboy will become **friends?** Why or why not?

3. What would you do if you discovered that you had **SECRET** powers?

WRITING PROMPTS

1. Pretend that you are also **working** at the ranch for the summer. Write a letter to a friend at home about what you've done and what you've seen.

2. How did Henry get to the ranch? Write a chapter that explains how he found the cowboy.

3. At the end of this book, Henry and the cowboy are **flying.** What do you think happens next? Write about it.